THIS BOOK BELONGS TO

children's choice®

IRA SLEEPS OVER

by BERNARD WABER

Houghton Mifflin Company, Boston

for Mark, Wendy and Amy

I was invited to sleep
at Reggie's house.

Was I happy!

I had never slept at a
friend's house before.

But I had a problem.
It began when my sister said:

"Are you taking your teddy bear along?"

"Taking my teddy bear along!" I said.
"To my friend's house? Are you kidding?
That's the silliest thing I ever heard!
Of course, I'm not taking my teddy bear."

And then she said:

"But you never slept without
your teddy bear before.
How will you feel sleeping without
your teddy bear for the very
first time? Hmmmmmmm?"

"I'll feel fine.
I'll feel great.
I will probably love sleeping
without my teddy bear.
Just don't worry about it," I said.

"Who's worried?" she said.

But now, she had me
thinking about it.
Now, she really had me
thinking about it.

I began to wonder:
Suppose I won't like
sleeping without my
teddy bear.

Suppose I just hate
sleeping without my
teddy bear.

Should I take him?

"Take him," said my mother.
"Take him," said my father.

"But Reggie will laugh," I sa[i]
"He'll say I'm a baby."

"He won't laugh," said my mother.
"He won't laugh," said my father.

"He'll laugh," said my sister.

I decided not to take my teddy bear.

That afternoon, I played with Reggie.
Reggie had plans, big plans.
"Tonight," he said, "when you come to my
house, we are going to have fun, fun, fun.
First, I'll show you my junk collection.
And after that we'll have a wrestling matc[h]
And after that, a pillow fight.
And after that we'll do magic tricks.
And after that we'll play checkers.
And after that we'll play dominoes.
And after that we can fool around with
my magnifying glass."
"Great!" I said. "I can hardly wait."

"By the way," I asked, "what do you
think of teddy bears?"

But Reggie just went on talking and planning as if he had never heard of teddy bears.

"And after that," he said, "do you know what we can do after that — I mean when the lights are out and the house is really dark? Guess what we can do?"

"What?" I asked.

"We can tell ghost stories."

"Ghost stories?" I said.

"Ghost stories," said Reggie, "scary, creepy, spooky ghost stories."

I began to think about my teddy bear.

"Does your house get
very dark?" I asked.
"Uh-huh," said Reggie.
"Very, very dark?"
"Uh-huh," said Reggie.
"By the way," I said again,
"what do you think
teddy bears?"

Suddenly, Reggie was in a big
hurry to go someplace.
"See you tonight," he said.
"See you," I said.

I decided to take my teddy bear.

"Good," said my mother.
"Good," said my father.

But my sister said:

"What if Reggie wants to know your teddy
bear's name. Did you think about that?
And did you think about how he will laugh
and say Tah Tah is a silly, baby name,
even for a teddy bear?"
"He won't ask," I said.
"He'll ask," she said.

I decided not to take my teddy bear.

At last, it was time to go to Reggie's house.

"Good night," said my mother.

"Good night," said my father.

"Sleep tight," said my sister.

I went next door where Reggie lived.

That night, Reggie showed me his junk.
He showed me his flashlight, his collection
of bottle caps, a chain made of chewing gum wrappers,
some picture postcards, an egg timer, jumbo goggles,
a false nose and mustache, and a bunch of old
rubber stamps and labels from his father's office.

ATTENTION
ATTENTION
PERSONAL AND CONFIDENTIAL
PERSONAL AND CONFIDENTIAL
PERSONAL AND CONFIDENTIAL

URGENT

VOID

VOID

AIR MAIL

SECOND NOTICE

PLEASE

PLEASE DO NOT FOLD

CANCELL

CANCELLED

CANCELLED

NOT PAID

Date _____

Checked _____

DUPLICATE

RUSH

DUPLICATE

DUPLICATE

DUPLICATE

FIRST CLASS

FIRST CLASS

SPECIAL DELIVER

THIS SIDE UP

We decided to play "office" with
the rubber stamps.

After that we had a
wrestling match.

And after that we had
a pillow fight.

And after that Reggie's father said:

"Bedtime!"

"Already?" said Reggie.
"Already," said his father.
We got into bed.
"Good night," said Reggie's father.
"Good night," we said.

Reggie sighed.

I sighed.

"We can still tell ghost stories," said Reggie.

"Do you know any?" I asked.

"Uh-huh," said Reggie.

Reggie began to tell a ghost story:

"Once there was this ghost and he lived in a
haunted house only he did most of the haunting
himself. This house was empty except
for this ghost because nobody wanted to
go near this house, they were so afraid of
this ghost. And every night this ghost would
walk around this house and make all kinds
of clunky, creeky sounds. *Aroomp! Aroomp!*
Like that. And he would go around looking for
people to scare because that's what he liked
most to do: scare people. And he was very
scary to look at. Oh, was he scary
to look at!"

Reggie stopped.

"Are you scared?" he asked.

"Uh-huh," I said. "Are you?'

"What?" said Reggie.

"Are you scared?"

"Just a minute," said Reggie,

"I have to get something."

"What do you have to get?" I asked.
"Oh, something," said Reggie.
Reggie pulled the something out of a drawer.
The room was dark, but I could see it had fuzzy arms
and legs and was about the size of a teddy bear.
I looked again. It was a teddy bear.

Reggie got back into bed.

"Now, about this ghost . . ." he said.

"Is that your teddy bear?" I asked.

"What?" said Reggie.

"Is that your teddy bear?"

"You mean this teddy bear?"

"The one you're holding," I said.

"Uh-huh," Reggie answered.

"Do you sleep with him all of the time?"

"What?" said Reggie.

"Do you sleep with him all of the time?"

"Uh-huh."

"Does your teddy bear have a name? Does your teddy bear have a name?" I said louder.

"Uh-huh," Reggie answered.

"What is it?"

"You won't laugh?" said Reggie.

"No, I won't laugh," I said.

"Promise?"

"I promise."

"It's Foo Foo."

"Did you say 'Foo Foo'?"

"Uh-huh," said Reggie.

"Just a minute," I said, "I have
to get something."
"What do you have to get?" Reggie asked.
"Oh, something," I answered.

The next minute, I was ringing my own doorbell.
The door opened.
"Ira!" everyone said. "What are you doing here?"
"I changed my mind," I answered.
"You what!" said my mother.
"You what!" said my father.
"You what!" said my sister.
(She was still up.)
"I changed my mind," I said. "I decided
to take Tah Tah after all."

I went upstairs.

Soon, I was down again
with Tah Tah.

My sister said:

"Reggie will laugh.
You'll see how he'll laugh.
He's just going to fall
down laughing."

"He won't laugh," said my mother.
"He won't laugh," said my father.

"He won't laugh," I said.

I came back to Reggie's room.
"I have a teddy bear, too," I said. "Do you
want to know his name?"
I waited for Reggie to say, Uh-huh.
But Reggie didn't say, Uh-huh.
Reggie didn't say anything.

I looked at Reggie.
He was fast asleep. Just like that,
he had fallen asleep.
"Reggie! Wake up!" I said. "You have
to finish telling the ghost story."
But Reggie just held his teddy bear
closer and went right on sleeping.

And after that —
well, there wasn't anything to do
after that.
"Good night," I whispered to Tah Tah.
And I fell asleep, too.